Boo and Ted's Amazing Adventures
Trying New Things

Written by John Dunn
Illustrated by Holly Withers

Copyright © 2025 by John Dunn

All rights reserved. No part of this publication may be reproduced, distributed, or transmitted in any form or by any means, including photocopying, recording, or other electronic or mechanical methods without prior written permission from the publisher, except in the case of brief quotations embodied in critical reviews and certain other noncommercial uses permitted by copyright law.

ISBN 978-1-7364223-8-0 (hardcover)
ISBN 978-1-7364223-9-7 (paperback)

For permission requests or ordering information, contact:

John Dunn
2358 University Avenue Box 434
San Diego, CA 92104
johndunn20@gmail.com

Follow Boo and Ted on Instagram @johndunnbooks

Book design by the Virtual Paintbrush.

Boo loves trying new things.

Ted . . .

does . . .

not.

"Hey Ted, this new dog food is delicious!! You should try it. It's fish!" barked Boo.

"I've never had fish," Ted replied. "It smells strange. I don't think I'd like it very much. I like chicken WAY better."

"But how do you know if you've never tasted it? Just give it a try, Ted, even if it's different."

Ted took an itsy-bitsy, teeny-tiny, little-bitty nibble.

"HEYYYYYYYYYY – this is tasty!!"

GOBBLE! CHOMP! MUNCH! SLURP!

"Time for your swim lesson," Mama called out.

"Whaatttttt!!!" exclaimed Ted. "But I don't know how to swim! I'll get water up my nose. I might even drown!!!!!"

"Ted, we're both learning," replied Boo. "I'll be there with you. Just give it a try, even if you're scared."

Ted gripped the side of the pool. The water was so deep, and the other side looked so far away!

He slowly let go . . .

Splish, Splash, Splish, Splash

"Look at me!" exclaimed Ted.
"I can doggie paddle!"

"This is so much fun!" Ted shouted. "Last one to the other side is a rotten egg!"

"Hey Ted, wanna ride bikes?"

"Nope. I don't know how to ride a bike. I might get lost! I might get a flat tire. I might even fall off!!"

"We can learn together. Think of all the dog parks we can bike to. Just try it, even if it might be hard."

"You almost have it Ted," Boo encouraged. "You just have to keep trying."

Ted pedaled slowly as the bicycle wobbled. He pedaled a little faster. The bike gathered speed . . .

Wheeeeeeeeeeeeeeeee!

"I'm glad you kept trying and didn't give up, Ted."

"Me tooooooooooooooo!" Ted shouted as he sped away.

"Bon Jovi is so awesome," said Ted as he hummed his favorite tune.

"You know what Ted, we should learn to play the guitar."

"No thanks, Boo. I've never played a guitar before. Besides, it looks hard. Why are there so many strings anyway?"

"We can jam together. Wouldn't that be so cool?" said Boo. "Just give it a try, even if it's new."

"I tried a new food, I tried swimming, and I tried riding a bike. I ended up liking all three," Ted thought to himself.

"I guess I can try the guitar too."

"Whoa oh, diggin up the roses
Dirt feels so good, tic-k-ling our noses
Whoa oh, diggin up the roses
Enjoy it now, before Mama notices
Whoa oh, diggin up the roses diggin up the roses."

"Ted, you coming to Barney's birthday party?"

"No thanks, Boo," Ted replied, shaking his head. "I won't know anyone there. I won't know how to play any of the games. I don't even like cake."

"You know Barney. He's our friend. Spot will be there too. It will be fun. Just give it a try, even if you're not sure."

Ted nervously clutched Barney's present as he and Boo walked to the park.

"What a great party," smiled Ted.

"Smacking the cat piñata is awesome, but so tiring," panted Boo.

"Pin the tail on the squirrel is the best!" yelled Ted.

"I hope the Vet gives us a treat," said Boo.

"The Vet? What's that?!?" cried Ted.

"That's our doctor," explained Boo. "She'll give us a checkup, look at our teeth, and maybe give us a shot or two."

"I don't wanna go," whimpered Ted. "I'm scared of shots. The needles are big. I bet it will hurt."

"I know it's scary. I'm nervous too," agreed Boo. "But the Vet makes sure we're healthy. The shots will keep us well. Staying healthy is important. You have to give it a try, even if you're afraid."

Ted squeezed Boo's paw as the Vet got the shot ready . . .

"All done," said the Vet.

"Wait? What?" Ted opened his eyes.
"Done?! But I barely felt anything."

"We were both really brave," replied Boo with a smile.

"You know what, we *were* brave," Ted answered thoughtfully.

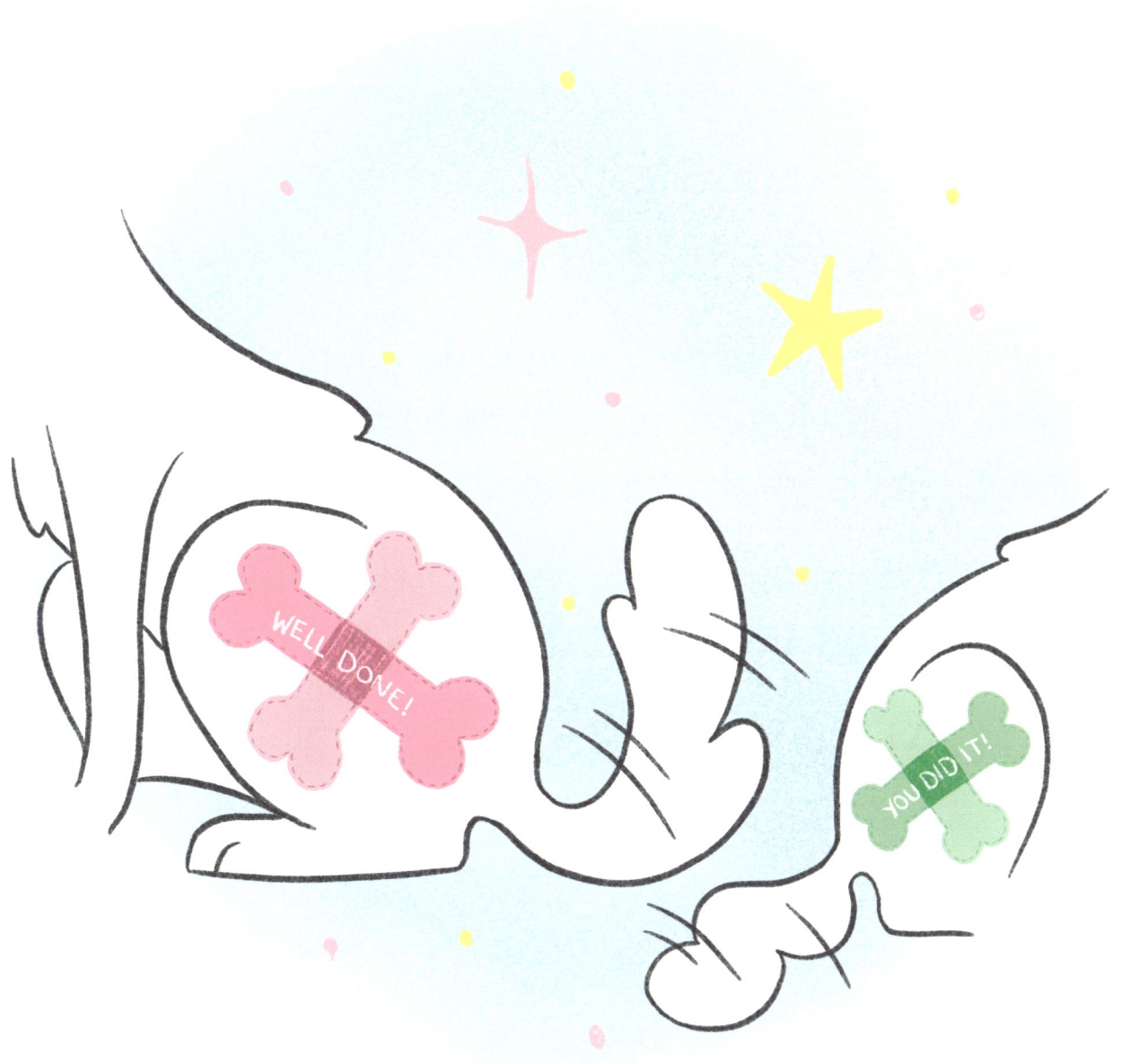

"I can't wait until the other dogs see our cool bandages," he added.

"Hey Ted, tomorrow's the first day of school. I'm so excited!"

"Oh No! Do we have to go?" groaned Ted. "I won't know any of the other dogs. I don't even know how to roll over yet! The other dogs might laugh at me."

"Actually," Ted paused and sniffled, "I think I'm coming down with a really bad cold."

AH AH AH AH CHHOOOOOO!

"Everyone will be nervous, Ted. It's the first day of school. We'll make new friends. And we'll learn new tricks. Just give it a try, even if you're worried."

Ted slowly walked into the entrance . . .

"I was nervous to go to Barney's party.

I was really scared to go to the Vet.

But I was brave. I went to both. Barney's party was fun and the Vet wasn't so bad," Ted remembered to himself.

"I can be brave and go to school, too!"

"School is great!" exclaimed Ted. "Our teacher is so nice and that book about the dog and his ball was so on point."

"You know," Ted added thoughtfully, "I'm really glad I didn't let being scared keep me from going to school."

"Hey Boo, let's go surfing today," said Ted.

"I didn't know you knew how to surf, Ted?"

"I don't, but . . ."

"YAAHOOOOOOOOOOOOOOOOOO!!"

The End

Made in the USA
Columbia, SC
21 December 2024

50388317R00020